THE DREAM C⟶
DAZZI⟶

In this book you'll find two stories about extraordinary animals – a cat who catches a star and a dream camel who becomes real!

Diana Hendry is the author of numerous stories for young readers, such as *Fiona Finds Her Tongue* (shortlisted for the Smarties Prize), *Midnight Pirate*, *Hetty's First Fling*, *Kid Kibble* (1992) and another Walker Double – *The Dream Camel and the Dazzling Cat*. She has also written two novels – *Double Vision*, for young adults and *Harvey Angell*, winner of the 1991 Whitbread Children's Novel Award. In her spare time she enjoys wearing interesting hats and spinning plates! She lives in Bristol with her son, daughter and piano.

05366

For Anne Kernighan

"Friendship is like the camel: once started
there is no way of stopping it." *Flaubert*
(A Camel Called April)

For Amy Green
(The Carey Street Cat)

First published 1990 as *A Camel Called April* and 1989 as
The Carey Street Cat by Julia MacRae Books

This edition published 1992 by
Walker Books Ltd, 87 Vauxhall Walk
London SE11 5HJ

Reprinted 1992

Text © 1989, 1990 Diana Hendry
The Carey Street Cat: illustrations © 1989 Barbara Walker
A Camel Called April: illustrations © 1990 Elsie Lennox
Cover illustration © 1992 Selina Young

Printed and bound in Great Britain by
Richard Clay Ltd, Bungay, Suffolk

British Library Cataloguing in Publication Data
A catalogue record for this title is available
from the British Library.
ISBN 0-7445-2303-6

The Dream Camel
and the Dazzling Cat

◆ DIANA HENDRY ◆

Includes
A Camel Called April
illustrated by Elsie Lennox

The Carey Street Cat
illustrated by Barbara Walker

WALKER BOOKS
LONDON

CONTENTS

A Camel Called April

The Carey Street Cat

A Camel Called April

Chapter 1

In the middle of the city was a square. Golden Square.

In the middle of the square was a park. Vagary Park.

Tall trees grew in the park and tall houses grew all around the square and in one of these houses lived Harold Arnold Percival Pemberton Yorick, otherwise known as Harry.

Harry was six. He lived at Number 12 Golden Square and from his bedroom window he had a very fine view of the park. He could see the curly-headed Scots Pine trees, the

Lebanon Cedar tree that was like a big, dark umbrella and the tall poplar trees that were like giants' brooms. He could see the swings and the paddling pool and the hut where the park gardener kept his spades and rakes. He could see the fountain where the dogs liked to pause for a drink and the benches where the old

people liked to sit and gossip. He could see the sloping avenues between the poplar trees where Jem Brewer on his skateboard 'Ratbones' and Charlie Piggot on his skateboard 'Gnash' went zig-zagging home.

Harry was the sort of boy who asked 'What if' a lot. What if there was a magic skateboard that could skate you from here to China in half a minute? What if the Scots Pines grew so tall they touched the clouds? What if the fountain fountained lemonade?

And Harry had amazing dreams. It rained jelly babies in Harry's dreams. Birds swam, fishes flew and lollipops grew on trees in Harry's dreams. But the really strange dreams began that spring, just after Harry had had chicken pox.

Harry dreamt a lion. And when he woke up and looked out of the window at the park – there it was, prowling about the climbing frame. On top of the climbing frame were four businessmen, one typist and two nurses who had been walking through the park on their way to work when the lion appeared.

There was a great hullabaloo in the square. Police cars wailed their sirens. A fire engine came wha-wha-wha-wha-wha-wha-ing up the road. There were anxious faces at every window and a police car with a megaphone on its roof drove round and round the square saying, "PLEASE STAY IN YOUR HOUSES. NOBODY IS TO COME OUTSIDE. A LION HAS ESCAPED FROM THE ZOO. PLEASE STAY IN YOUR HOUSES."

The park gardener climbed onto the roof of his hut. Harry could see his legs trembling.

Harry looked very carefully at the lion. Of course it must have escaped from the zoo. But what if . . ? What if it hadn't escaped from the zoo but from Harry's dream?

Very soon four lion-keepers arrived from the zoo. They threw the lion an enormous hunk of meat and while he was eating it, the smallest lion-keeper crept up and gave the lion an injection in his bottom. The lion staggered a bit as if he was drunk and then fell down, fast asleep and snoring. The other lion-keepers wrapped him in a big net and carried him off to the van. Everyone cheered.

The four businessmen, one typist and two nurses climbed down from the climbing frame and went off to work. The firemen had to help the gardener off the roof. Everything was quiet again in Vagary Park in Golden Square.

But the next night Harry dreamt a hippopotamus. And in the morning there it was, wallowing in the paddling pool and looking rather surprised. People were not so

frightened of a hippopotamus. A group of children on their way to school stood around the pool feeding the hippopotamus with apples and cakes from their packed lunches.

The zoo men were there again – the hippopotamus-keepers this time. One of them was arguing with the gardener.

"This is very careless of you," said the gardener, "losing animals like this. First a lion. Now a hippopotamus."

"Now look here," said the hippopotamus-keeper with his hands on his hips. "This hippopotamus isn't our hippopotamus. We counted ours this morning. Both of them. And they are still there. We don't know where this hippopotamus came from and if you don't mend your manners we'll leave him here!"

They had to get a crane to winch the hippopotamus into a big tank of water and then they had to winch the tank onto a lorry.

The next night Harry dreamt of monkeys. And there they were in the morning having a lovely time, swinging from poplar tree to poplar tree and climbing to the very top of the Scots pines.

The people in Vagary Park were getting used to strange animals now. They looked out of their windows and said, "Oh! It's monkeys this morning!" and carried on with their breakfasts.

The monkey-keepers from the zoo were very angry. The park gardener

was very worried. Why did all these animals come to *his* park? The monkeys were hard to catch. The zoo men had to go to the baker and buy an enormous bag of buns to tempt the monkeys down out of the trees.

Harry thought it was time he confessed.

The gardener and the zoo men were gazing up at the tallest pine tree when Harry arrived. Two monkeys were dropping pine cones on their heads.

"Excuse me," said Harry.

"We're very busy just now, lad,"

said the zoo man without looking at Harry. "We're trying to catch these 'ere monkeys."

"I'm afraid they're *my* monkeys," said Harry turning very red.

The zoo man did look at Harry then. "No jokes, lad," he said, "what do you mean they're *your* monkeys?"

"I dreamt them," said Harry.

"You dreamt them!" echoed the zoo man laughing and patting Harry's head.

"Yes," said Harry. "*And* I dreamt the lion and the hippopotamus."

"I wish I was dreaming," said the zoo man digging into his bag for another bun. "Now run along, lad. We've got work to do here."

Harry turned away unhappily. But the gardener stopped him. The gardener was a short, stocky man who smoked a pipe. He had grey-green eyes, the colour of tree trunks. "You live over there, don't you?" he said, pointing to Harry's house.

"Yes," said Harry.

"I've seen you at the window and wondered why you weren't at school," said the gardener.

"I've had chicken-pox," said Harry. "And I *did* dream those animals. Really I did."

"Well, maybe you did and maybe you didn't," said the gardener, "but off you go now while we catch the rest of these monkeys."

That night Harry dreamt a giraffe. There it was in the morning, nibbling the tops off the pine trees. This time the gardener didn't call for the zoo man. Instead he knocked on Harry's door.

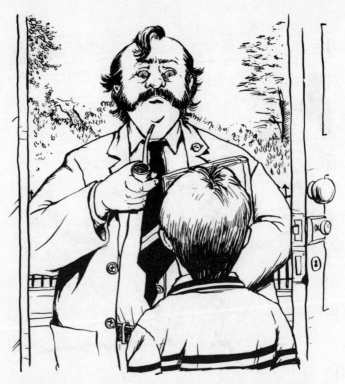

"Yes," said Harry, "I know. There's a giraffe in the park. I dreamt him there last night."

"Look," said the gardener puffing thoughtfully on his pipe, "I've got an idea. Do you think you could try and dream the giraffe back to where he came from?"

"I could try," said Harry doubtfully. "Where *do* giraffes come from?"

"Africa," said the gardener. "I've brought you a book with pictures of Africa in it. Look at it before you fall asleep and see if you can dream this giraffe back into Africa."

So that night Harry lay in bed with pictures of the African bush and giraffes. And it was quite easy! He dreamt of lots of giraffes in a safari park and the dream giraffe of Vagary Park lolloped off to join them.

"There you are!" said the gardener the next morning. "That's saved me a lot of bother. But I'm a bit tired of animals now. Do you think you could try dreaming me some really fine roses or a nice bed of delphiniums?"

"I'll try," said Harry. And when he went to bed that night he took with him a gardening book full of pictures of roses and delphiniums.

But he didn't dream of roses and delphiniums.

Harry dreamt a camel.

Chapter 2

And there it was in the park the next morning. A rather beautiful camel with a single tufted hump, long, knobbly-kneed legs, long eye-lashes, a soft and gentle mouth and a stringy bit of a tail.

The camel liked it in the park. She liked the avenues between the poplar trees, the paddling pool and the bar across the top of the swings because this was a good place on which to scratch her itchy chin.

The gardener came rushing to Harry's door.

"Where're my roses?" he cried. "Where're my delphiniums? And why have I got a camel instead?"

"I'm terribly sorry," said Harry. "I did try to dream about roses and delphiniums but April just drifted in."

"April!" shrieked the gardener.

"That's her name," said Harry apologetically.

"Look," said the gardener, puffing deeply on his pipe, "do you think you could try and have a nap this morning – a quick forty winks perhaps – and dream this camel – this April – back again? Dream of the Sahara desert. That's where camels live. Dream lots and lots of sand."

"I'll try," said Harry. But even though he curled up on his bed and snuggled his ted, he didn't feel a bit sleepy. When he went over to the park to tell the gardener this, he found that April had fallen asleep underneath the Lebanon Cedar and the gardener was sitting beside her eating his sandwiches.

"I'm just not sleepy. I'll try tonight," said Harry. "A desert you said?"

"Yes. The Sahara desert," said the gardener, saving a few crusts for April. He had tethered her to the Lebanon Cedar and quite a crowd of children had gathered round to look at her.

"Can we have a ride please, mister?" asked one boy.

"This camel isn't for riding. It's just here on a visit. It's going back to the Sahara tonight," said the gardener.

"Cor! That's a long way!" said the boy.

"She's going by air," said the
gardener loftily. "Tomorrow she'll
just vanish – like a dream! You'll
see!"

"Pity we can't have a ride," said
the boy and he wandered away.

That night Harry went to bed with a book about nomads and their camels travelling through the Sahara. Camels, he learnt, were called 'ships of the desert'.

And Harry *did* dream of April. In his dream April said, "I like your dream, Harry. Dreams are as big as deserts. I can wander about your dreams forever. I think I'll stay in your dreams at night and spend my days in the park."

"You can't do that!" said Harry (in his dream). "Camels don't belong in English dreams. They belong in African deserts."

"I don't care," said April. "I like it here. We camels have very independent minds you know. You can't just push us about." And with that the camel sat down. And although Harry prodded her and talked nicely to her and said how happy she would be as a ship of the desert, April would not budge.

When Harry woke up, he rushed to his window to look out and there was April. She and the gardener were having breakfast together. The gardener was sitting on the In-Beloved-Memory-of-Mary-Loder bench and April stood behind him, nibbling his hair now and again and helping him out with his cornflakes.

Harry forgot his own breakfast and rushed over to the park.

"Hello," said the gardener. "What happened to your dream of the Sahara?"

"I did dream a desert," said Harry sitting down beside him on the bench, "but April wouldn't go. She said my dream was as big as a desert only

more fun and she was going to stay."

April bent down her long snaky neck at this and tried nibbling a piece of Harry's hair. She didn't like it.

"I'm not really surprised," said the gardener. "Camels are famous for being very stubborn. Sometimes the nomads have to light fires underneath them to get them to move on."

"I wouldn't like to do that," said

Harry, "not even in a dream."

At this point April, who had been chewing a piece of poplar tree and turning it round and round in her mouth, spat.

"That's something else camels are famous for," said the gardener happily. "Spitting."

"Well, what are we going to do?" asked Harry. "Are you going to call the zoo?"

The gardener stroked April's nose. "No, not this time," he said. "The truth is I've taken rather a shine to April. A man needs something that's a bit dream-like in his life, something a bit strange and not-quite-of-this-world."

April flashed her long eyelashes at both of them.

"I was thinking I'd keep her," said the gardener. "In fact sitting here on the Beloved Memory bench, I thought to myself – what if I built a camel house next to my hut?"

"What a wonderful idea!" said Harry.

But just at that moment a very large gentleman with a fat, important stomach came striding across the park. He was wearing a bowler hat and carrying an umbrella. Behind him was a policeman.

"Excuse me," said the fat gentleman, "my name is Fred Knobbs and I am Chairman of the Parks Committee. It has come to my attention that you are keeping a camel in the park. This is not allowed. That camel will have to go." And Mr Knobbs pointed his umbrella at April.

April bent down her snaky neck and very gently removed Mr Knobbs's bowler hat.

Chapter 3

"It doesn't say anything in the Park
Rules about not allowing camels,"
said the gardener. He pointed to a
board at the entrance to the park.
The rules were very old. The
gardener read them aloud.

1. No person shall stand, sit, lie
    upon or walk over any flower
    bed.
2. No person shall play or take
    part in any game except on the
    space allotted therefore.
3. No person shall at any time
    drive or bring into the park

any horse, donkey, cattle, sheep or pig.

"There you are," said the gardener, "nothing about camels." (I'm very glad I didn't dream a pig, thought Harry.)

Mr Knobbs waved his umbrella angrily at the Park Rules. "Well, of

course it doesn't mention camels," he cried. "Camels aren't English are they? When those rules were made nobody thought of camels. But if they had, they would have been on the list. In fact I shall see to it that they are added to the list. Tomorrow."

"Actually," said Harry, "this camel isn't a real camel. It's a dream camel."

Mr Knobbs glared at Harry. "Now boy," he said, puffing up his stomach and looking more important than ever, "you can't make a fool out of me you know. I am Chairman of the Parks Committee. That is a Very Important Position. If that was a dream camel then I would be asleep.

And I'm not." Mr Knobbs pinched himself just to make sure. And then he pinched Harry because he felt so cross.

April looked at Mr Knobbs with her large eyes. She flapped her eyelashes a couple of times and then spat on Mr Knobbs's left shoe. Mr Knobbs went very red.

"Now, now," said the gardener, taking long soothing puffs on his pipe, "why don't we all sit down and talk this over?"

They all sat down on the In-Beloved-Memory-of-Mary-Loder bench. It seemed to make everyone calmer. April wandered off and lay down under the umbrella of the

Lebanon Cedar.

"I was wondering," said the gardener, speaking very slowly in between puffs on his pipe, "what if we put April – I mean the camel – to work? What if she made some money for Vagary Park – for all the parks?"

Mr Knobbs folded his hands over his stomach and laughed. "Dream

money, I suppose," he said.

"Well, no," said the gardener. "What I was thinking of was this. What if we kept the camel in the park and allowed people to have rides on her back? We could charge 20p a ride. They don't have a camel at the zoo. I'm sure people would come a long way to see a camel in a park."

"We could become the most famous park in England!" said Harry excitedly.

"Uuum!" said Mr Knobbs slowly and thoughtfully. "Uuum! The most famous park in England, eh?"

"Well, yes," said the gardener. "And I expect a Parks Committee that thought up such an idea would be quite famous too."

"They'd probably want to interview you on television," said Harry.

"On television, eh?" said Mr Knobbs smiling. "Me and the camel side by side. Both of us smiling."

"Yes," said Harry and the gardener together.

"She mustn't spit though," said Mr Knobbs anxiously.

"Oh no!" said the gardener. "We'd arrange that. You see she's not park trained yet. But I'll have a word with her about spitting."

"I shall go and arrange an Extraordinary General Meeting of the Parks Committee," said Mr Knobbs standing up. "You will be hearing

from me shortly." And he marched
away swinging his umbrella very
happily.

Harry and the gardener did a little
dance together round and round the
fountain. April watched them. She
thought dancing was very silly.

Chapter 4

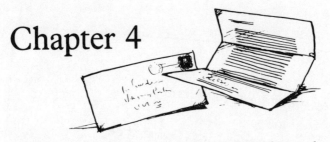

Two days later a letter arrived at the gardener's hut. This is what it said.

Dear Gardener and Harry,

We had a very long Committee
Meeting about your camel, April.
We have decided that we would
like April to stay in Vagary Park
and to become Camel-in-Residence.
She will give the children rides
during the summer and you can
build a camel house next to the
hut. The Committee would like to
have a party in the park so that
April can be made properly
welcome.

Yours greenly,

B. knobbs.

B.Knobbs, Chairman
P.S. We think it should be 30p a ride.

Harry and the gardener had another dance round the fountain.

"You can stay, April!" said Harry, giving the camel a big hug. April closed one eye and winked.

The Parks Committee arranged a big party to welcome April as Camel-in-Residence of Vagary Park. All the committee came and all the people who lived in Golden Square. Jem Brewer came on 'Ratbones' and Charlie Piggot came on 'Gnash'. A special saddle had been made for April. It had brightly coloured leather tassels and on either side of it were three wooden seats so that April could carry six children at once. It was called a howdah. "Now she's a

ship of the park," said Harry.

At the party the children were given free rides. Harry and the gardener walked about looking very proud (but not quite as proud as Mr Knobbs who was given the first ride on the camel and photographed wearing his special gold chain so that everyone knew he was Chairman of the Parks Committee).

April settled down very happily at Vagary Park. She liked to follow the gardener about while he was digging the flowerbeds or mowing the lawns. She became very friendly with the park regulars and they became very fond of her.

The gardener built her a tall house next to his hut and she used it when the weather was bad. But she didn't need it at night because then she drifted off, on her long, knobbly-kneed legs, into Harry's dreams.

Harry didn't always see her in his dreams. There were some nights when he knew that April was there –

but she was asleep in a corner of his dream. Those dreams were like plays in which April didn't have a part. On some nights, when April was feeling homesick for the desert, she and Harry would dream themselves into the Sahara and Harry would ride on her back over miles and miles of sand. Sometimes April would interrupt a dream when she found it boring.

So many children wanted a ride on April's back that the Parks Committee made a lot of money and they bought new roses and delphiniums and new swings for parks that didn't have any swings.

The rules on the board at the

entrance to the park were changed.
Rule number three now said this:

> No person shall at any time
> drive or bring into the park
> any horse, donkey, cattle,
> sheep or pig. But a camel is all
> right.

In the middle of the city was a square
called Golden Square. In the middle
of the square was a park called
Vagary Park. In the middle of the
park was a camel called April.

THE CAREY STREET CAT
Chapter 1

Jenkins was the Carey Street cat.
He belonged to everyone in general
and no-one in particular.

It had not always been so. Once
upon a time, when Jenkins was a
small stray kitten, unsteady on his
legs, he belonged to Mrs Thumble.
Mrs Thumble lived at Number 2
Carey Street and she found Jenkins
mewing on her doorstep and
looking very lost. Jenkins was small
and neat and as black and shiny as
a new LP record. Mrs Thumble
took him in and gave him sops of

bread in milk. "You're a pretty little thing," she said, "you can live with me if you like."

And at first Jenkins *did* like living with Mrs Thumble. He had his own basket in the kitchen and he felt safe and cosy. But as he grew up, Mrs Thumble noticed that Jenkins had very long straight legs and that he could leap from the table to the

top of the dresser and from the floor
to the top of the fridge; he was a
high-leaping cat.

Jenkins practised his high jumps
all over Mrs Thumble's house. He
jumped from the bed to the top of
the wardrobe. He jumped from the
window-sill to the top of the
bookcase. He jumped from the top
to the bottom of the stairs. By the
time the summer came, Jenkins felt
brave and adventurous and full of
beans – jumping beans. He climbed
all the trees and he jumped all the
garden walls of Carey Street from
2 to 12 and back again. And he
felt very proud of himself indeed.

It was while he was jumping the

garden walls that Jenkins decided that it might be nicer to have more than one home. Mrs Thumble was very kind to him of course, but old Mr Drubbs (at Number 8) gave him bacon rinds for breakfast and the Hobjoy children (at Number 6) gave him little cubes of cheese. At Number 10 lived Miss Turner, the piano teacher, and she let Jenkins lie in a patch of sunshine in her front room while she played him a tune. She said it was called 'Kitten on the Keys'.

Jenkins liked variety. He liked having his breakfast at Number 8, his lunch at Number 6 and his tea at Number 2. And he very much

liked a lot of people making a lot of
fuss over him. Jenkins was a very
happy cat that summer.

But the people of Carey Street
were not so happy. They quarrelled
about Jenkins.

They all met together outside the
Tak Kee Chip Shop (which was the
meeting place in Carey Street) and

Mrs Thumble said that Jenkins belonged to her because she had found him on her doorstep.

"Finder's keepers," said Mrs Thumble and she shook her walking stick at Mr Drubbs.

"That's as may be," said Mr Drubbs, "but I think Jenkins has

chosen to live with me. We have breakfast together every morning."

The Hobjoy children all hopped up and down and chanted a rhyme:

"Jenkins belongs to us!
Nobody else
Loves him as much!
If we don't have him
We'll scream and we'll fuss!"

Miss Turner, who was very shy and who *never* made a fuss, said quietly, "I think Jenkins likes my house best. I think he's a most musical cat. He listens very carefully when I practise my scales."

It was Harry who suggested that they all share Jenkins. Harry knew how Jenkins felt because Harry had two homes. From Monday to Thursday Harry lived with his mum at Number 4 Carey Street and from Friday to Sunday he lived with his dad at Number 12 Carey Street. Harry had grown to like it that way.

So while they were all quarrelling about Jenkins, Harry said, "Why don't we share him?"

Mrs Thumble stopped waving her walking stick, the Hobjoy children stopped hopping, Miss Turner stopped wringing her long piano fingers, Mr Drubbs stopped

scowling and they all looked at
Harry.

"Why don't we share him?" said
Harry again. "Jenkins can be the
Carey Street cat."

"Well," said Mrs Thumble, "I
suppose I do get quite tired of
Jenkins' high jinks. I think it's a
nice idea."

"I think it's lovely!" said Miss
Turner. "It's *dolce* and *alimando*!"

"I don't know about that," said Mr Drubbs, who didn't like people to be cleverer than he was, "but I agree."

"We agree, too," said the eldest of the Hobjoy children. "Only it would be nice if Jenkins came to us on a Saturday when we're home from school."

And so it was decided that Jenkins should be the Carey Street cat, and after a while the people of Carey Street enjoyed sharing him. Mrs Thumble and Mr Drubbs, who had never been friendly before, often met in the café on the corner to compare notes on how high Jenkins could jump.

Mr Drubbs said, "I've seen him
jump from the garden wall to the
roof."

And Mrs Thumble said, "I've
seen him jump from the roof to the
top of the cherry tree at Number
12."

Harry often went round to Miss
Turner's and sat on her sofa with
Jenkins purring in his lap while

Miss Turner played 'Kitten on the Keys'; and the Hobjoy children visited Mrs Thumble so that she could tell them again about the day she found Jenkins on her doorstep.

The people of Carey Street were very proud of Jenkins' high jumps, but none of them – not even Harry – had quite bargained for Jenkins jumping so high that he caught a star. Sharing a cat was one thing, sharing a star was quite another.

Chapter 2

It happened one midsummer night.
Jenkins was at the top of the cherry
tree in Harry's dad's garden,
swaying up and down among the
summer blossom. On a warm night
it was his favourite sleeping place,
for Jenkins liked to be close to the
stars.

He had never caught one before.
Jenkins had caught three mice (at
Miss Turner's), a lot of runaway
cotton-reels (at the Hobjoys) and
lots of flying autumn leaves, but
never a star.

It was not a whole star, just the tiniest piece of star dust, what Harry called afterwards 'a little-bit-of-Dazzle'. As Jenkins swayed up and down in the cherry tree, the little-bit-of-Dazzle separated itself from all the other stars in the sky and drifted down, down, down. Jenkins fixed his bright green eyes on it and a special kind of midsummer magic went straight to his high-leaping heart. With one exceptionally high jump – as if his legs had springs in them – Jenkins leapt up, up, up through the darkness. He caught the star in his mouth, dropped down through the night and landed neatly and prettily, all four paws together, on the wall of Number 12.

A thrill and a tail-curling shiver went through Jenkins as he caught the little-bit-of-Dazzle. He laid it carefully on the wall. It tasted nicer than cod, nicer than Whiskas, nicer than bacon rind, nicer than anything. It was delicious and beautiful and Jenkins loved it with all his heart.

He took it back up to the top of
the cherry tree and hung it over a
bough like a piece of Christmas
tinsel. He slept beside it, opening
one magicked green eye every now

and again to make sure it was still
there, still dazzling. In the morning
he would show it to all the people of
Carey Street. How proud they
would be that he, Jenkins the Carey
Street cat, had caught a star!

In the morning the Dazzle was even more dazzling. It hadn't switched itself off in daylight like the rest of the stars. Out of the sky it seemed to have lost the knack. It shone on the cherry tree as if Christmas Day was every day. Jenkins purred over it. He licked it lovingly. He could hardly wait for the people of Carey Street to wake up so that he could show them his treasure of the night.

He decided to begin with Mrs Thumble. She had, after all, been the first in Carey Street to give him a home. She deserved a first look at the Dazzle.

Jenkins climbed down from the

cherry tree, holding the Dazzle very carefully in his mouth, jumped the garden walls from 12 to 2, leapt onto the window-sill of Mrs Thumble's kitchen window and waited.

At seven-thirty Mrs Thumble came downstairs in her dressing gown and slippers to make herself a cup of tea. But at the kitchen door she stopped. What was it? A terribly bright light shone through the window and filled the whole kitchen. It was weird! It was scary! It was far, far too bright! Mrs Thumble thought an Unidentified Flying Object had landed in her garden overnight. And then she saw Jenkins and his star.

"Ooooooh!" shrieked Mrs Thumble. "Jenkins! You bad, bad cat! You've gone and caught a star! Oooh! Away! Shoo! Vamoooosh!" And Mrs Thumble pulled down her kitchen blind with a great snap.

Jenkins was astonished. And insulted. He turned tail as snootily as he could (it was quite difficult on

a window-sill), picked up the star
very delicately, and leapt two walls
to the Hobjoys' house.

The littlest Hobjoy was out in the
garden practising cartwheels. She
took one look at Jenkins and his
Dazzle, opened her mouth wide and
howled. Still howling she ran into
the house. Mr Hobjoy came rushing
out with a fire-extinguisher. He

tried to douse Jenkins and his star –
but Jenkins leapt, just in time.

He did no better with Miss
Turner. She was practising her
early morning scales when Jenkins'
star shone through her window.
Miss Turner was very frightened.

She thought an angel had come to
earth and she got down on her
knees, shut her eyes and said her
prayers.

Harry's mum saw Jenkins and his star and she looked very cross and drew the curtains. "That cat," she said (for it was a Tuesday and Harry was there), "is just like your father. After the impossible. He thinks he's so grand he can play with the stars. He thinks he's some kind of a magic creature – well he's only a cat." And Harry's mum shook her head and tut-tutted.

But Harry thought Jenkins was more than just a cat. Harry thought Jenkins was partly a cat and partly a magic creature and he peeped through the drawn curtains at him. The little-bit-of-Dazzle was so dazzling that Harry couldn't help smiling.

"If I could jump like Jenkins can jump, I think I'd jump for a star, too," said Harry.

"High jumps come before a fall," said his mother.

"A Dazzle like that might be worth a fall," said Harry. But Harry's mum did not agree. "I'm not going to have anything to do with that cat until he puts that star back," she said. And the curtains of Number 4 stayed firmly closed.

Jenkins was very upset. If only they could each have a little lick of the bit-of-Dazzle they would know what a thrilling, tingling, magical thing it was. They would all live happily ever after. But they wouldn't even look.

Jenkins went back to the cherry tree, hung up his bit-of-Dazzle and looked at it sadly. He could not bear to give it up. He loved it as a mother cat loves her kitten. If the Dazzle had had ears Jenkins would have licked behind them.

Very soon not only everyone in Carey Street knew that Jenkins had caught a star, but the whole town knew. Reporters came from the newspapers and heard all about Jenkins' high jumps. *The Daily Tizz* said he could leap sixty feet and *The Daily Twist* said he could leap a hundred feet. They tried to

take photographs of Jenkins and his star but it was too bright for their cameras.

A television crew came and interviewed all the Carey Street people.

"I'm sure I saw an angel," said
Miss Turner. "I think an angel
came to Carey Street and left
behind this little-bit-of-Dazzle and
Jenkins found it."

Mr Drubbs became very
important. He stuck his thumbs in
his waistcoat pockets and said, "Of
course, I've known from the
beginning that Jenkins was an extra

special cat."

A Professor of Cats came to look at Jenkins. "I think he is evolving into a new kind of bird," said the Professor.

(Harry looked up 'evolving' in his mother's dictionary. It meant 'to develop into'. Harry very much hoped that Jenkins wasn't going to develop into a bird. He liked him as a cat.)

On the radio a man from Upper Barming said that he was very worried in case Jenkins got into the habit of catching stars and then there wouldn't be any left in the sky.

Overnight Jenkins was famous and unhappy. Everyone was talking about him but no-one in Carey Street seemed to love him any more. There was not a single saucer of milk put out on a single doorstep that night. Not a snitch of bacon rind, not a scrap of fish. No-one called, "Good-night Jenkins!" No-one said, "See you in the morning, Jenkins!"

Jenkins and his star were alone. Or at least that is what Jenkins thought. Jenkins didn't know about Harry and Harry's plan.

Chapter 3

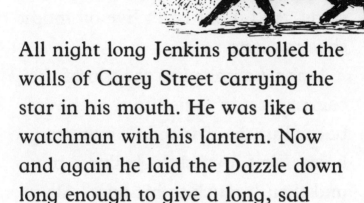

All night long Jenkins patrolled the walls of Carey Street carrying the star in his mouth. He was like a watchman with his lantern. Now and again he laid the Dazzle down long enough to give a long, sad "EeeeOOOOOOWWWW..."

The truth was that Jenkins was very hungry. He was hungry for love and bacon rinds. The Dazzle was still delicious. Every time he licked it, it seemed to have a different flavour and it sent a magic shiver all down his spine and up his tail. But it wasn't filling. It wasn't filling like milk and Whiskas and Hobjoy cheese cubes and bacon rinds. And a cat can't live on magic shivers alone.

Jenkins climbed to the top of the cherry tree and tried to toss the star back. But the star didn't want to go back. First it stuck to Jenkins' paws and then it stuck to his nose. All

that licking had made it very sticky. Miserably Jenkins rocked himself to sleep in the boughs of the cherry tree. He didn't know that Harry, who could see the cherry tree from his bedroom window at Number 4, was watching him and making his plan.

The next day, although it was only Thursday, Harry went to see his dad.

Harry's dad was painting a picture. He was painting a picture of the cherry tree at night with Jenkins asleep and the Dazzle dangling beside him.

Harry looked at the painting and he said, "Isn't painting a picture of a star rather like trying to catch one?"

"Yes, it is a bit," said Harry's dad. "But all I can catch is the *idea*

of the star. My painted star won't be nearly as bright as the real thing. It won't sizzle and you won't be able to lick it."

"Jenkins is in a lot of trouble," said Harry.

"I know," said his dad.

"I saw him last night trying to toss the star back," said Harry, "but it wouldn't go. No-one in Carey Street will speak to Jenkins until the star is put back."

"Sometimes," said Harry's dad, "people and cats only learn how high they can jump by jumping too high."

"Miss Turner says you have to be prepared to get a piece of music wrong a lot of times before you get it right," said Harry.

"Yes. Well, it's much the same with jumping," said Harry's dad. "Jenkins will never jump quite so high again. He'll get his jumping right. He'll be more careful with his magic."

"So you *do* think Jenkins is magical?" said Harry.

"Everyone has some magic," said his dad. "You just have to learn to look after your own magic so that it doesn't carry you away. Jenkins got a bit carried away."

"I've been making a plan to help Jenkins," said Harry.

"Go on," said his dad.

"Well, I thought Jenkins needed someone to rescue him from the star."

"Um," said his dad, "a star, even a bit-of-Dazzle is a big responsibility for such a little cat."

"I thought perhaps someone could take the star and – and – er put it in a safe place," said Harry.

"Someone? You mean us?" said his dad.

"Yes," said Harry.

Harry's dad closed his eyes and thought for a long time. When he opened his eyes, he said, "I've got it. You come to my house tomorrow don't you, Harry?"

"Yes, it's Friday," said Harry.

"Well then, tomorrow night at midnight. Operation Jenkins. Bring lots of gloves."

Chapter 4

At midnight on Friday, Harry and his dad were ready for Operation Jenkins. Harry's dad carried a long ladder and a saucepan with a lid. Harry carried a small dish full of bacon rinds and cheese. They both wore sunglasses and two pairs of gloves each.

Out into the back garden they went – looking very like burglars – and down to the cherry tree. There was Jenkins, a sad and bedraggled Jenkins, and there was the Dazzle, gorgeous and glistening beside him.

"I'd love to keep it and hang it on the Christmas tree," whispered Harry.

"Well you can't," said his dad. Jenkins pricked up his ears. People! Carey Street people! And .... and .... yes! Bacon rinds! Without a second thought Jenkins leapt lightly out of the cherry tree and landed neatly on the lawn.

"There's a good cat!" said Harry, and Jenkins gobbled up the bacon rinds and cheese while Harry stroked him. Meanwhile, Harry's dad set the ladder against the tree and, holding the saucepan in one hand, he climbed the ladder until he

reached the Dazzle. (He was very glad of his sunglasses.) Quick as a flash – or quick as a Dazzle – he picked the star off the bough, dropped it into the saucepan of water and put the lid on it.

There was a long, slow, sighing, sizzling sound. 'Zizzzzzz' went the Dazzle. Jenkins looked up, meowed a little sadly, and carried on with the cheese.

Harry and his dad rushed back into the kitchen. Harry's dad set the pan on the table and poured in some plaster mix. "When the plaster's hard we'll take it out," he said.

They had a mug of milk each while they waited and Harry tried not to yawn. In half an hour the plaster had set hard and Harry's dad lifted it out of the saucepan.

"No-one would ever guess there's a star inside," said Harry. But his dad had picked up a chisel and was busy chiselling the plaster into the shape of a star. (He got it a bit wrong and the star ended up with six points instead of five, so that when Harry's mum saw it, she said, "That's just the sort of star

your father would make. A star
with six points instead of five.")

After that Harry got a small tin
of dark blue enamel paint, opened it
with a penny, and painted the star
until it was a dark, shiny blue.
Harry's dad made a hole in the sixth
point of the star and slid a chain
through the hole.

"There!" he said. "This is the Carey Street Star. Now for the last part of Operation Jenkins."

Jenkins had come in from the garden. He had jumped quietly into the rocking chair and fallen fast asleep.

Harry and his dad smiled at each other. They left Jenkins sleeping there and this time they went out of the front door – with Harry's dad carrying the ladder and Harry carrying the blue shiny star on its chain – and they went down Carey Street to the Tak Kee Chip Shop.

There was nobody about. Everybody in Carey Street was fast asleep. Harry's dad held the ladder

and Harry climbed up it until he
could loop the chain over the chip
shop sign-board. The sign-board
creaked a little bit and then the star
hung there as if it had always been
there and Harry climbed down the
ladder.

He and his dad shook hands.
Then they hugged each other.
Then they danced round and
round in the road trying not to
laugh or wake anyone up.

In the morning Mrs Thumble found Jenkins sitting on her window-sill again. "Oh, what a good cat you are," said Mrs Thumble. "You've put that star back." And she gave him a big saucer of top-of-the-milk.

It was the littlest Hobjoy who first saw the blue star hanging by the Tak Kee Chip Shop sign. She rushed home to tell all the other Hobjoys. Very soon everyone in Carey Street was out looking at the dark blue star.

"It's quite obvious what has happened," said Miss Turner. "The angel came back, took away the real star because it was too much for Jenkins – too much for all of us – and left us this one, as a reminder."

And because this was a rather nice story and because nobody wanted to upset Miss Turner, they all agreed that was what had happened. Harry and his dad had decided not to tell the real story and Jenkins couldn't tell it, although sometimes, on a moonlight night, he could be seen sitting above the

signboard of the chip shop, swinging to and fro with his eyes half-closed as if he was in a magic dream, remembering the Dazzle.

A strange thing happened to the chips at the Tak Kee Chip Shop. Harry's mum was the first to notice it. "These chips are heavenly," she said to Harry one night when they were having a fish and chip supper. "They have a sort of extra sizzle."

"Yes," said Harry, "they're magic!"

And Harry's mum gave him a funny sort of look and said, "Yes, you could be right."